This Orchard
book belongs to

_____

_____

_____

For Saffron and Barnaby
G.A.

This book is dedicated to Tony for his constant
support and good humour
D.W.

Publisher's note:
Many thanks to the Natural History Museum of London for their help with this book.

Pteranodon and Ichthyosaurus lived in the dinosaur era,
but they are not officially dinosaurs.

ORCHARD BOOKS
338 Euston Road, London NW1 3BH
Orchard Books Australia
Level 17/207 Kent Street, Sydney, NSW 2000
First published in 2004 by Orchard Books
First paperback publication in 2005
ISBN 978 1 84362 609 1
Text © Purple Enterprises Ltd, a Coolabi company 2004 **coolabi**
Illustrations © David Wojtowycz 2004
The right of Giles Andreae to be identified as the author and of David Wojtowycz
to be identified as the illustrator of this work has been asserted by them in
accordance with the Copyright, Designs and Patents Act, 1988.
A CIP catalogue record for this book is available from the British Library.
14 16 18 20 19 17 15 13
Printed in China
Orchard Books is a division of Hachette Children's Books,
an Hachette UK company.
www.hachette.co.uk

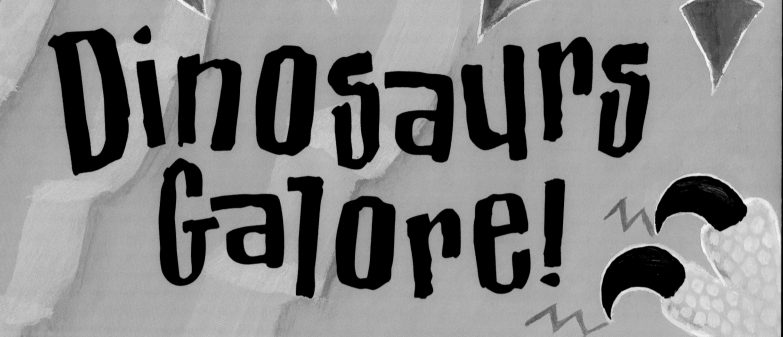

Dinosaurs Galore!

Giles Andreae ⬦ David Wojtowycz

ORCHARD

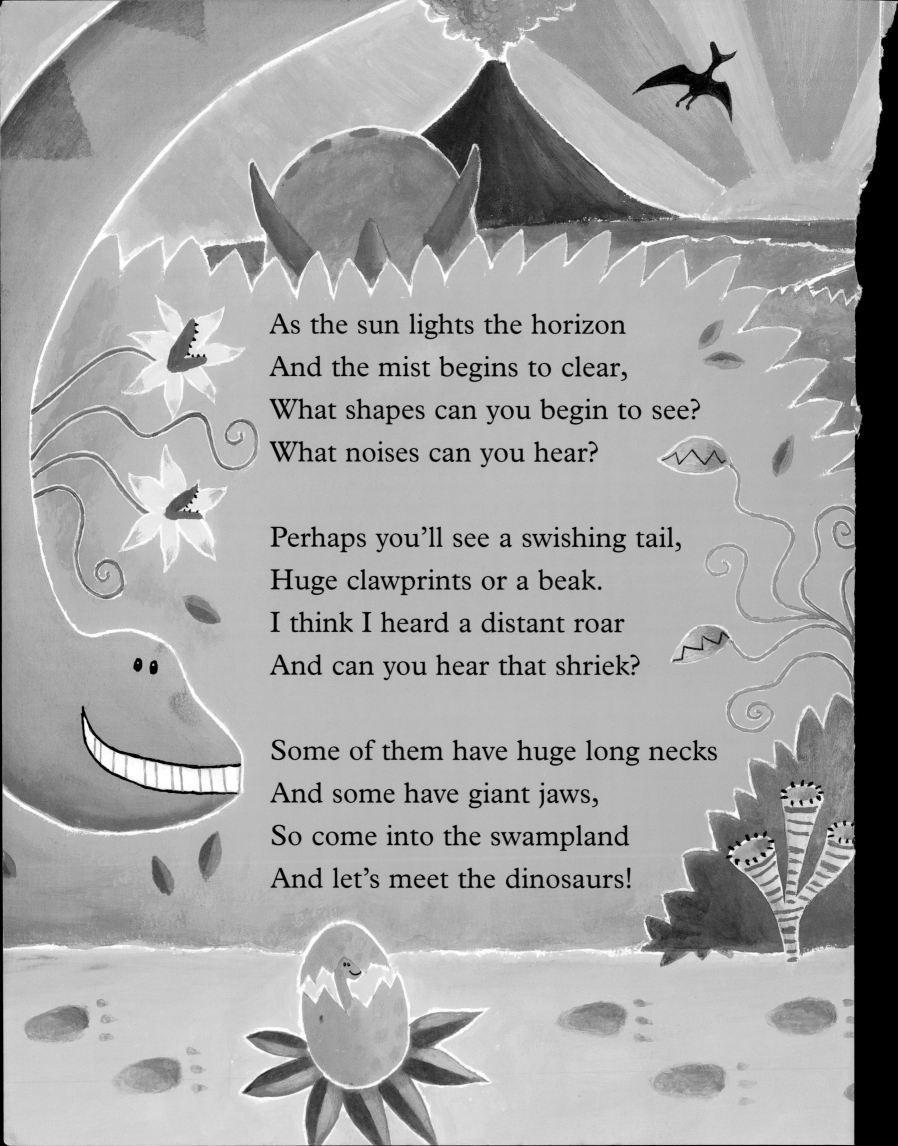

As the sun lights the horizon
And the mist begins to clear,
What shapes can you begin to see?
What noises can you hear?

Perhaps you'll see a swishing tail,
Huge clawprints or a beak.
I think I heard a distant roar
And can you hear that shriek?

Some of them have huge long necks
And some have giant jaws,
So come into the swampland
And let's meet the dinosaurs!

Tyrannosaurus Rex

(tie-RAN-oh-sore-us REX)

I'm big and strong and scary
But I'm very pleased to meet you,
Because my giant gaping jaws
Are very keen to EAT YOU!

Ankylosaurus
(an-KIE-loh-sore-us)

I've got armour on the top of me
And armour underneath,
So if you try to eat me up
You'll probably break your teeth!

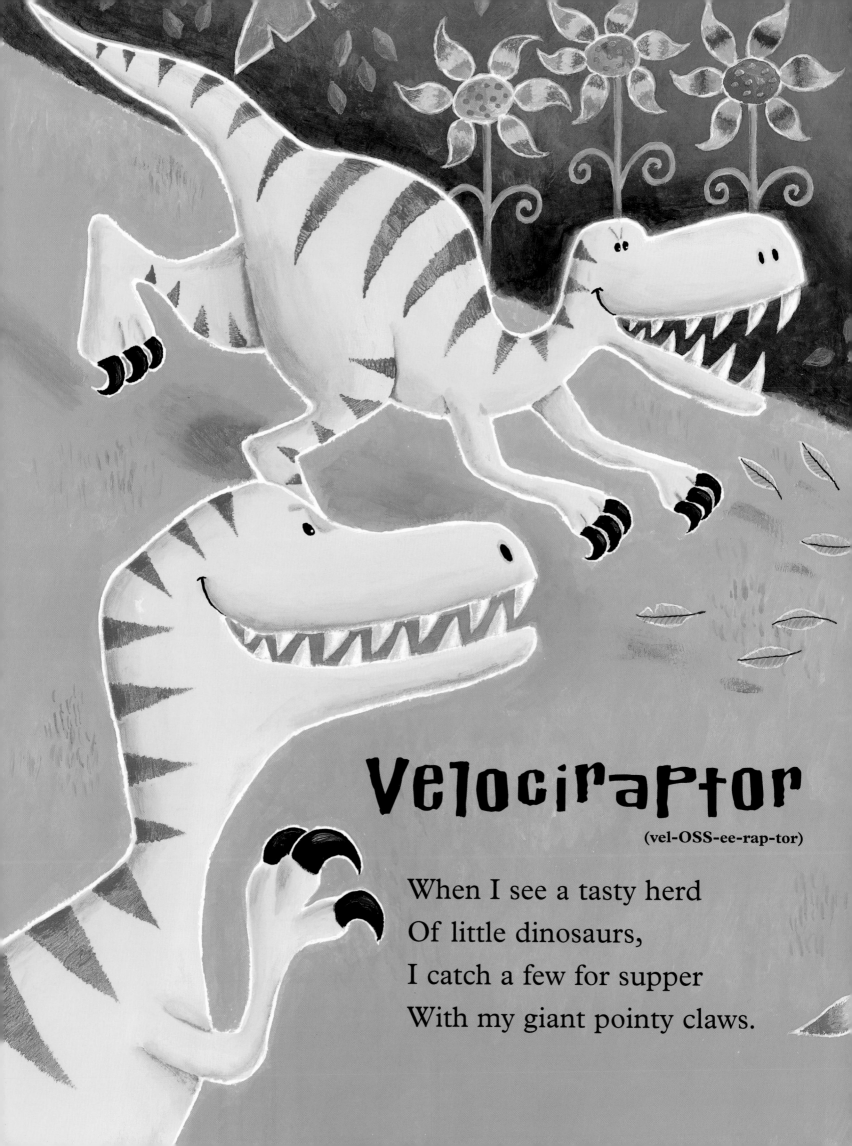

Velociraptor

(vel-OSS-ee-rap-tor)

When I see a tasty herd
Of little dinosaurs,
I catch a few for supper
With my giant pointy claws.

Microraptor

(mike-ROW-rap-tor)

I'm as little as a chicken
But please don't be too hasty,
Although I may be chicken-sized
I'm nothing like as tasty!

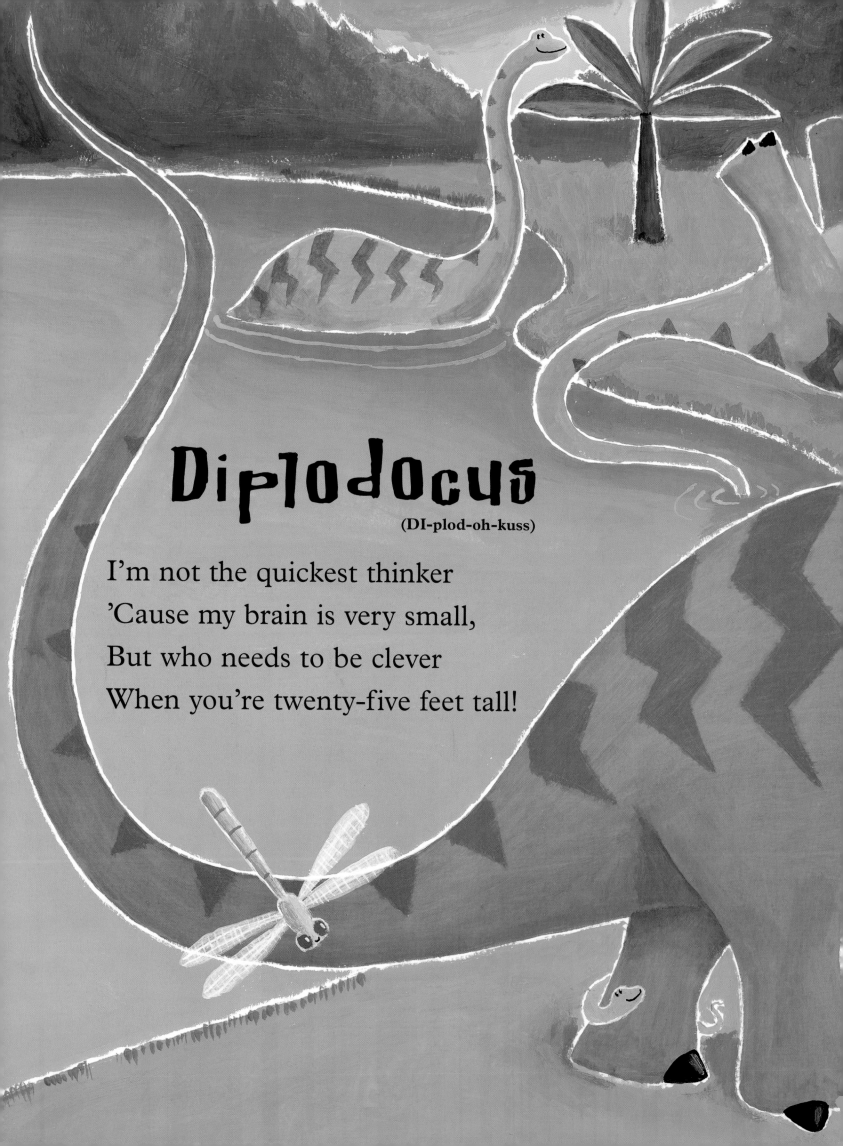

Diplodocus
(DI-plod-oh-kuss)

I'm not the quickest thinker
'Cause my brain is very small,
But who needs to be clever
When you're twenty-five feet tall!

Spinosaurus

(SPINE-oh-SORE-us)

I'm sure you can see the big sail on my back,
I use it for storing up heat.
It's also quite handy for making new friends
Because everyone says it looks neat!

Triceratops
(tri-SERRA-tops)

I'm the Triceratops, how do you do?
I've got these three horns on my head.
They're useful for keeping my enemies back
But they're not very comfy in bed!

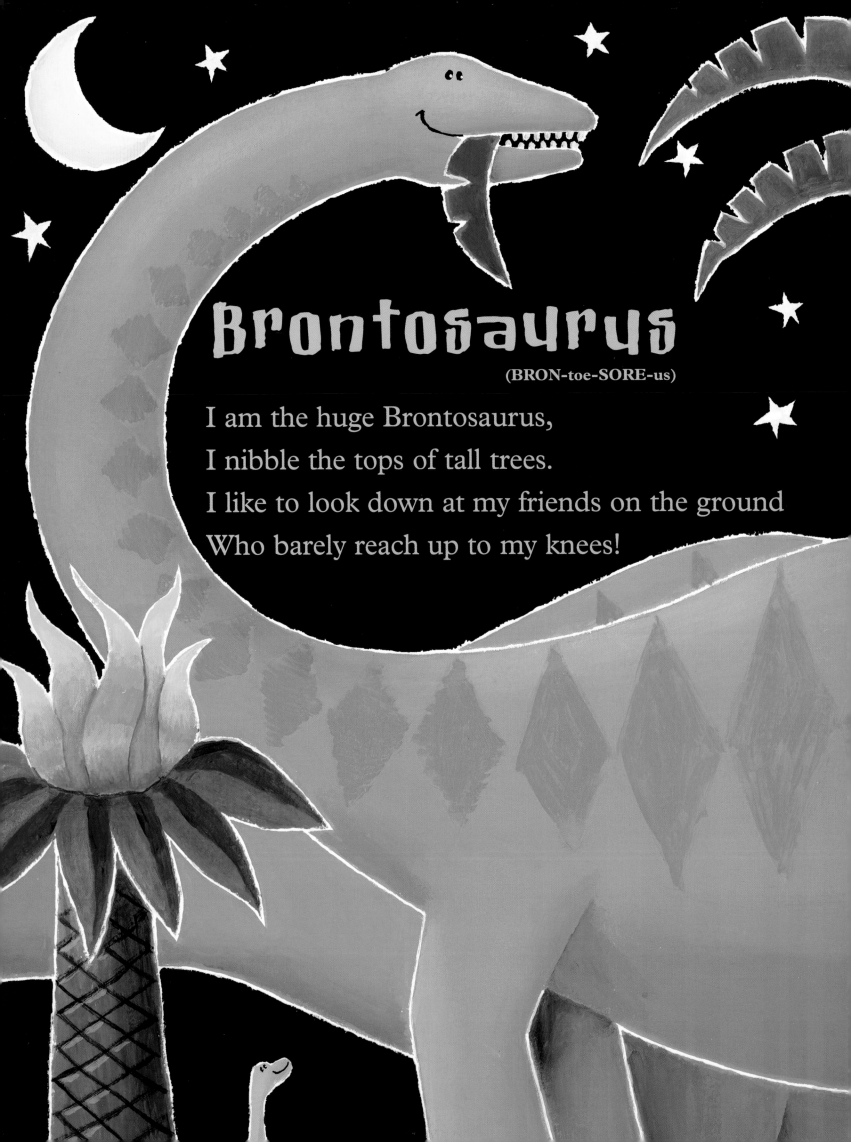

Brontosaurus

(BRON-toe-SORE-us)

I am the huge Brontosaurus,
I nibble the tops of tall trees.
I like to look down at my friends on the ground
Who barely reach up to my knees!

Pteranodon
(ter-AN-o-don)

See the crest upon my head
It helps me when I glide,
And the girls say it looks groovy
As I swoop from side to side!

Ichthyosaurus
(IK-thee-oh-SORE-us)

I'm the dolphin dinosaur
I live down in the sea,
And when I spot some scrumptious squid
I eat them up for tea!

Stegosaurus
(STEG-oh-SORE-us)

Hello, I'm the stout Stegosaurus
With two rows of plates down my back.
I've also got spikes on the end of my tail
Which I use when I'm under attack!

Giganotosaurus

(gig-an-OH-toe-SORE-us)

I am enormous and fierce and strong,
I live by the shores of the lake.
There's a rumbling sound
When I stomp on the ground,
And the earth starts to shudder and shake.

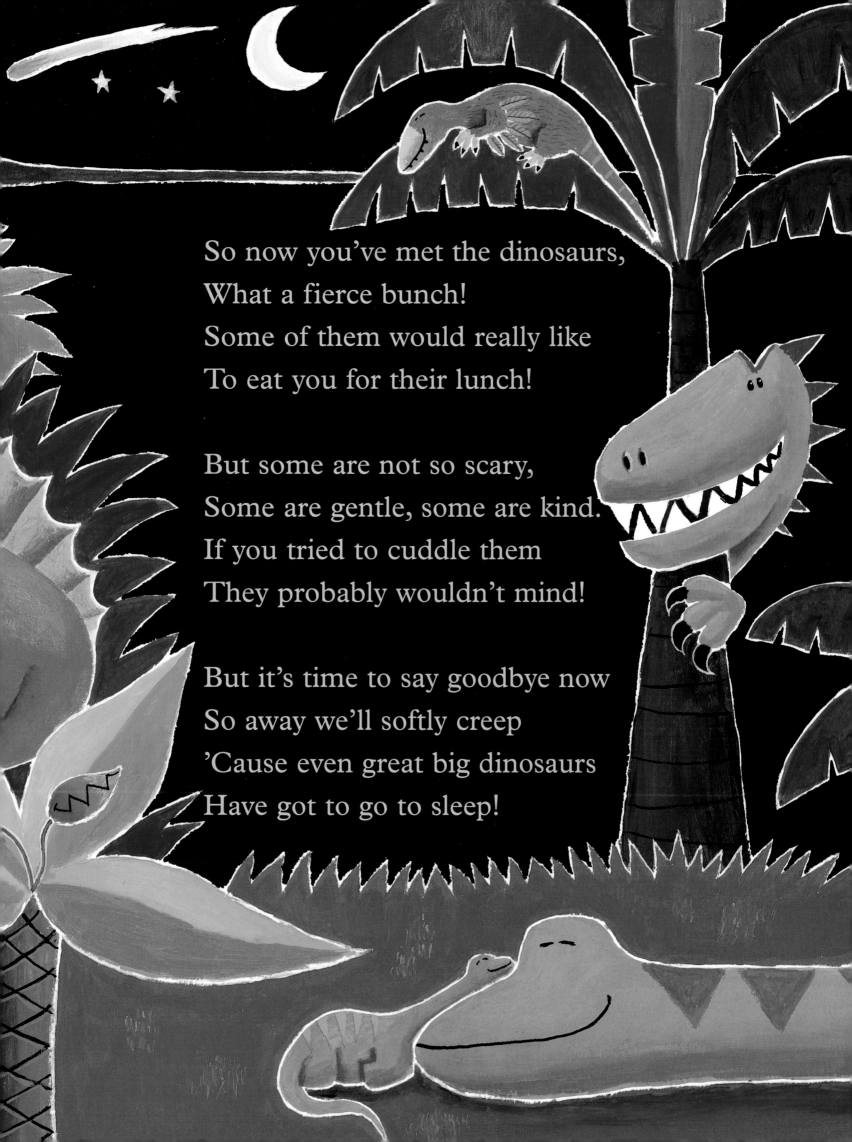

So now you've met the dinosaurs,
What a fierce bunch!
Some of them would really like
To eat you for their lunch!

But some are not so scary,
Some are gentle, some are kind.
If you tried to cuddle them
They probably wouldn't mind!

But it's time to say goodbye now
So away we'll softly creep
'Cause even great big dinosaurs
Have got to go to sleep!

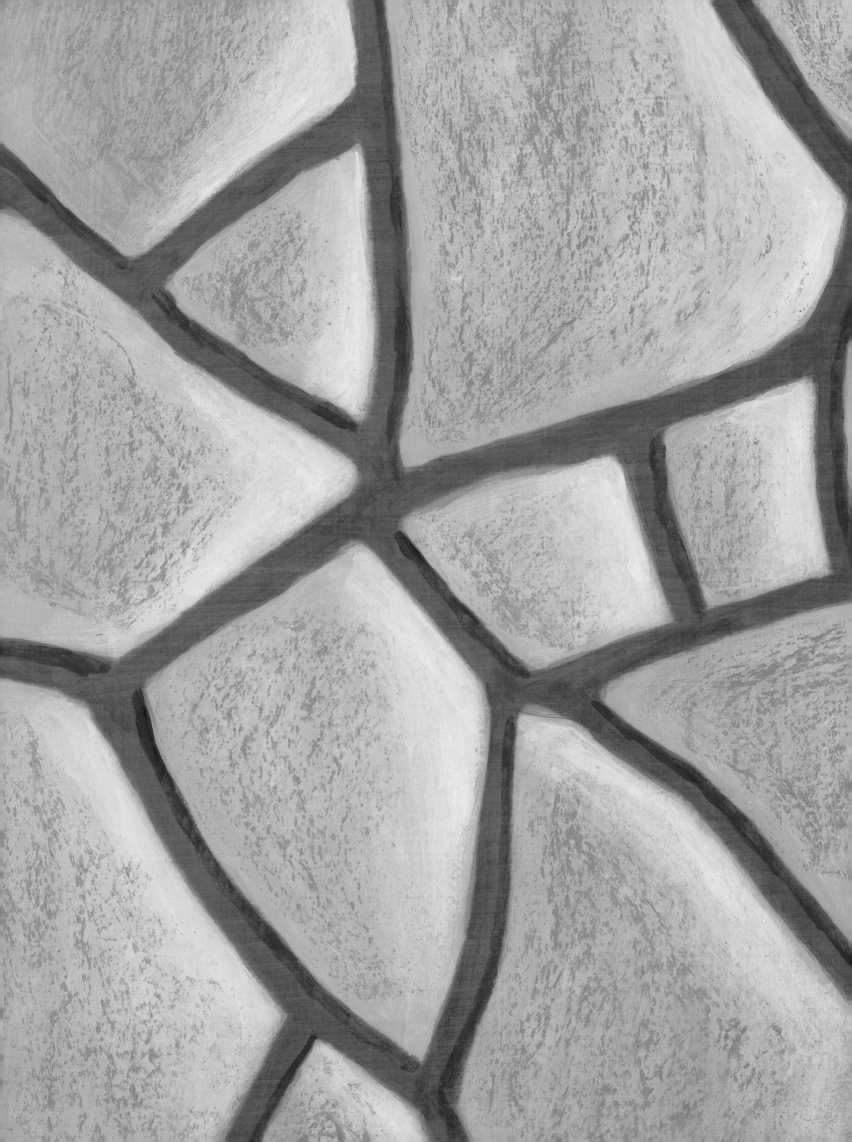